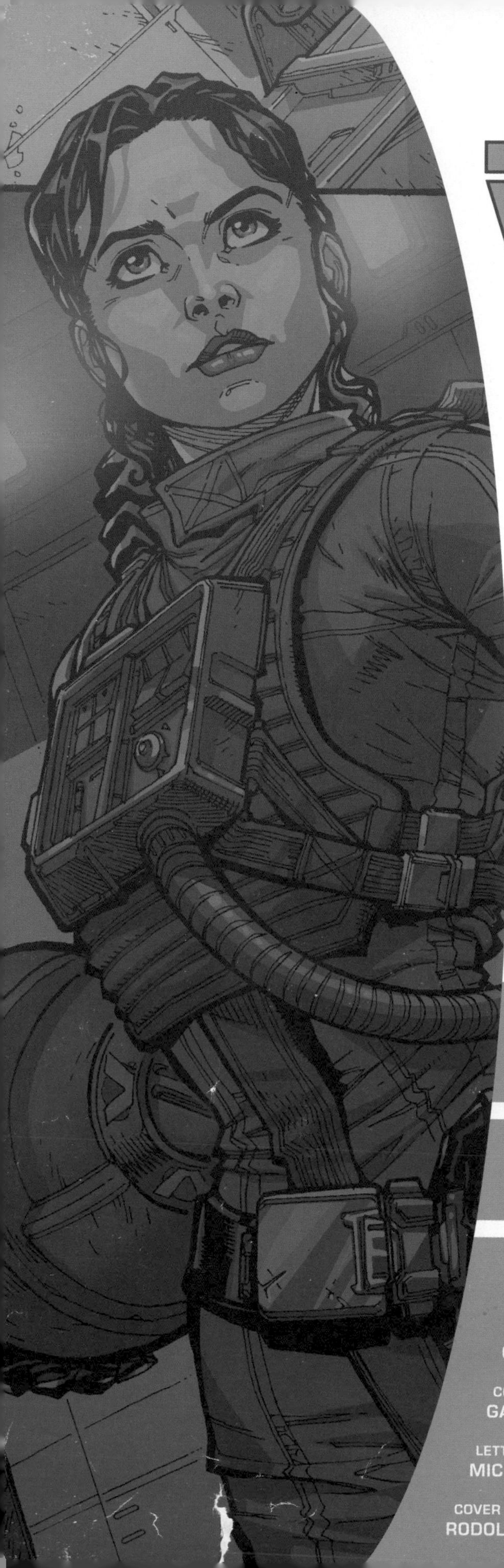

STAR WARS®

IN THE SHADOW OF YAVIN
VOLUME SIX

Their mission for the Rebels discovered, Han Solo and Chewbacca are being hunted through the Coruscant underworld by Boba Fett and Bossk. Help is offered from an unexpected source—but it comes with a huge price.

Grounded for breaking mission protocol, Luke Skywalker and fellow pilot Prithi further disobey orders after Luke receives a warning from the ghost of Ben Kenobi. They set out to locate fellow squad members Princess Leia, Wedge, and Tess . . .

. . . who are but a single hyperspace jump ahead of Colonel Bircher's Star Destroyer. Worse, Leia is injured, and her X-wing is severely damaged. With no hope in sight, the trio prepares for a last stand against the Empire . . .

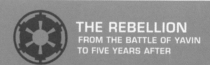

THE REBELLION
FROM THE BATTLE OF YAVIN TO FIVE YEARS AFTER

The events in this story take place shortly after the events in *Star Wars:* Episode IV—*A New Hope.*

SCRIPT
BRIAN WOOD

ART
CARLOS D'ANDA

COLORS
GABE ELTAEB

LETTERING
MICHAEL HEISLER

COVER ART
RODOLFO MIGLIARI

DARK HORSE COMICS

WWW.ABDOPUBLISHING.COM

Reinforced library bound edition published in 2015 by Spotlight, a division of ABDO
PO Box 398166, Minneapolis, Minnesota 55439. Spotlight produces high-quality
reinforced library bound editions for schools and libraries. Published by agreement
with Dark Horse Comics, Inc., and Lucasfilm Ltd.

Printed in the United States of America, North Mankato, Minnesota.
052014
072014

THIS BOOK CONTAINS
RECYCLED MATERIALS

STAR WARS: IN THE SHADOW OF YAVIN

LIBRARY OF CONGRESS CATALOGING-IN-PUBLICATION DATA

Wood, Brian, 1972-
   Star Wars : in the shadow of Yavin / writer: Brian Wood ; artist: Carlos D'Anda. --
Reinforced library bound edition.
      pages cm.
   "Dark Horse."
   "LucasFilm."
   ISBN 978-1-61479-286-4 (vol. 1) -- ISBN 978-1-61479-287-1 (vol. 2) -- ISBN 978-1-
61479-288-8 (vol. 3) -- ISBN 978-1-61479-289-5 (vol. 4) -- ISBN 978-1-61479-290-1
(vol. 5) -- ISBN 978-1-61479-291-8 (vol. 6)
1. Graphic novels. I. D'Anda, Carlos, illustrator. II. Dark Horse Comics. III. Lucasfilm,
Ltd. IV. Title. V. Title: In the shadow of Yavin.
   PZ7.7.W65St 2015
   741.5'973--dc23

                            2014005383

Spotlight

A Division of ABDO
www.abdopublishing.com

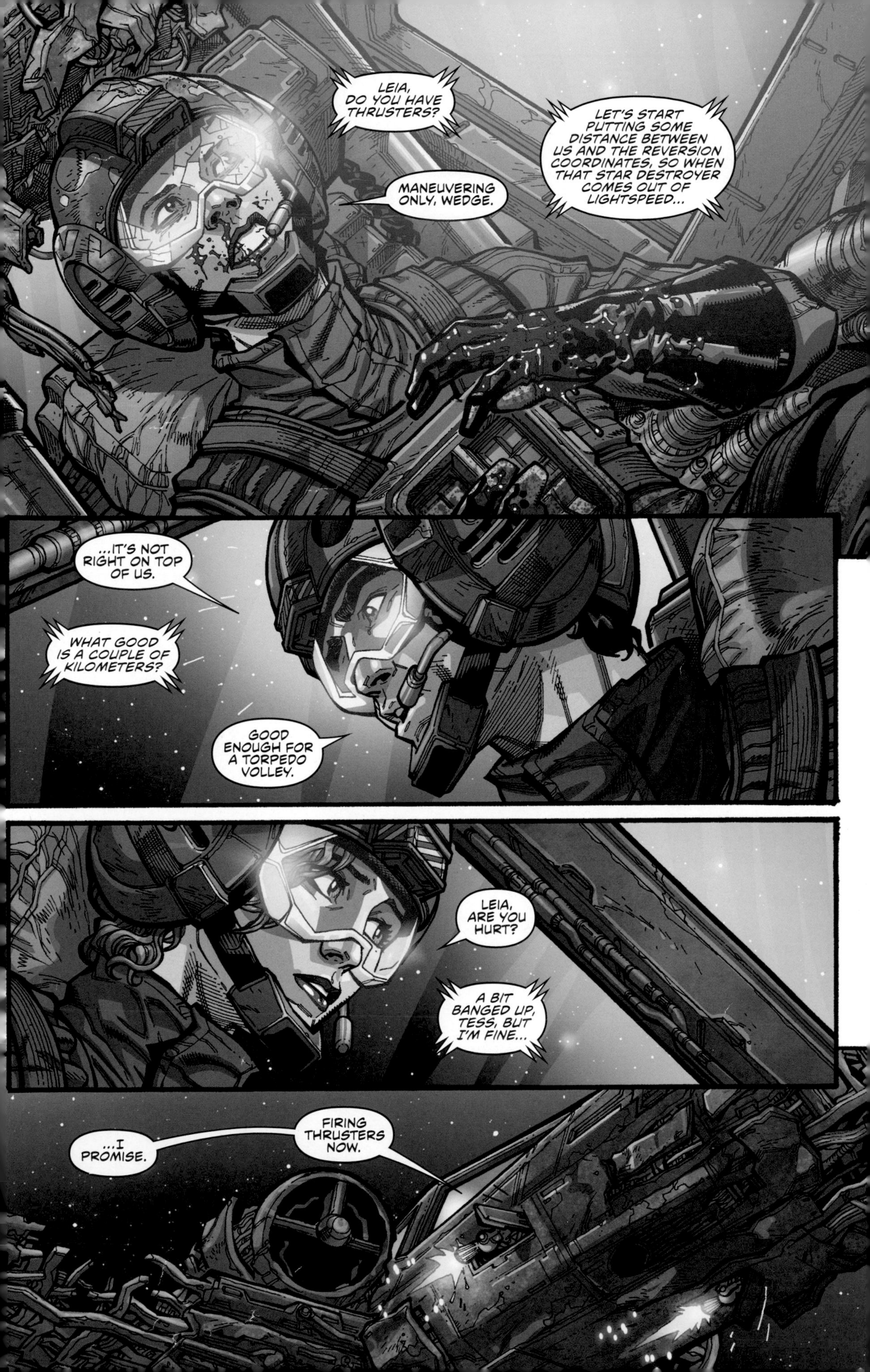
LEIA, DO YOU HAVE THRUSTERS?
MANEUVERING ONLY, WEDGE.
LET'S START PUTTING SOME DISTANCE BETWEEN US AND THE REVERSION COORDINATES, SO WHEN THAT STAR DESTROYER COMES OUT OF LIGHTSPEED...
...IT'S NOT RIGHT ON TOP OF US.
WHAT GOOD IS A COUPLE OF KILOMETERS?
GOOD ENOUGH FOR A TORPEDO VOLLEY.
LEIA, ARE YOU HURT?
A BIT BANGED UP, TESS, BUT I'M FINE...
...I PROMISE.
FIRING THRUSTERS NOW.

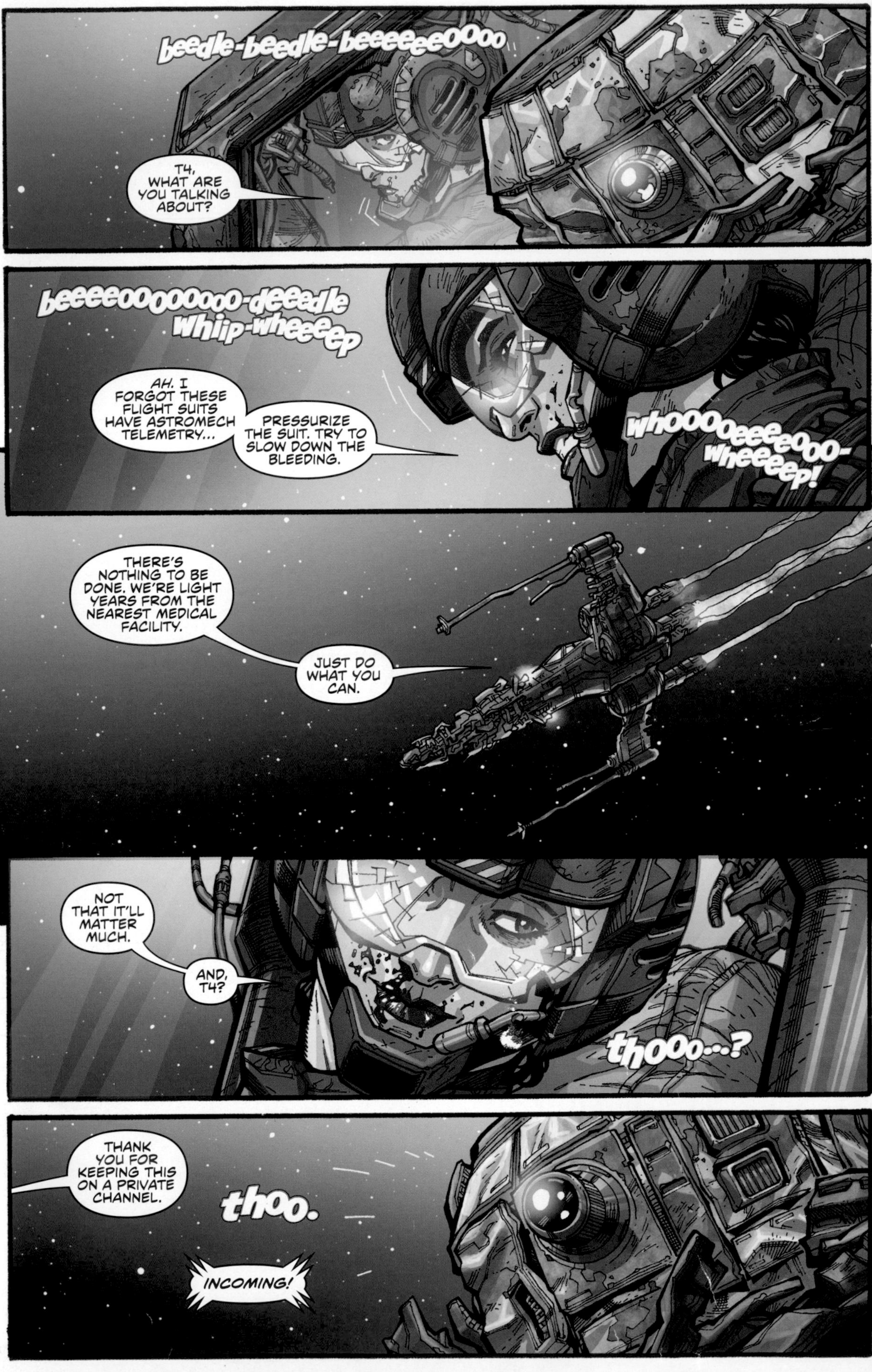
beedle-beedle-beeeeeeOOoo
T4, WHAT ARE YOU TALKING ABOUT?
beeeeOOOOOOo-deeedle whiip-wheeeeep
AH. I FORGOT THESE FLIGHT SUITS HAVE ASTROMECH TELEMETRY...
PRESSURIZE THE SUIT. TRY TO SLOW DOWN THE BLEEDING.
whoooOeeeeOOO-wheeeep!
THERE'S NOTHING TO BE DONE. WE'RE LIGHT YEARS FROM THE NEAREST MEDICAL FACILITY.
JUST DO WHAT YOU CAN.
NOT THAT IT'LL MATTER MUCH.
AND, T4?
thooo...?
THANK YOU FOR KEEPING THIS ON A PRIVATE CHANNEL.
thoo.
INCOMING!

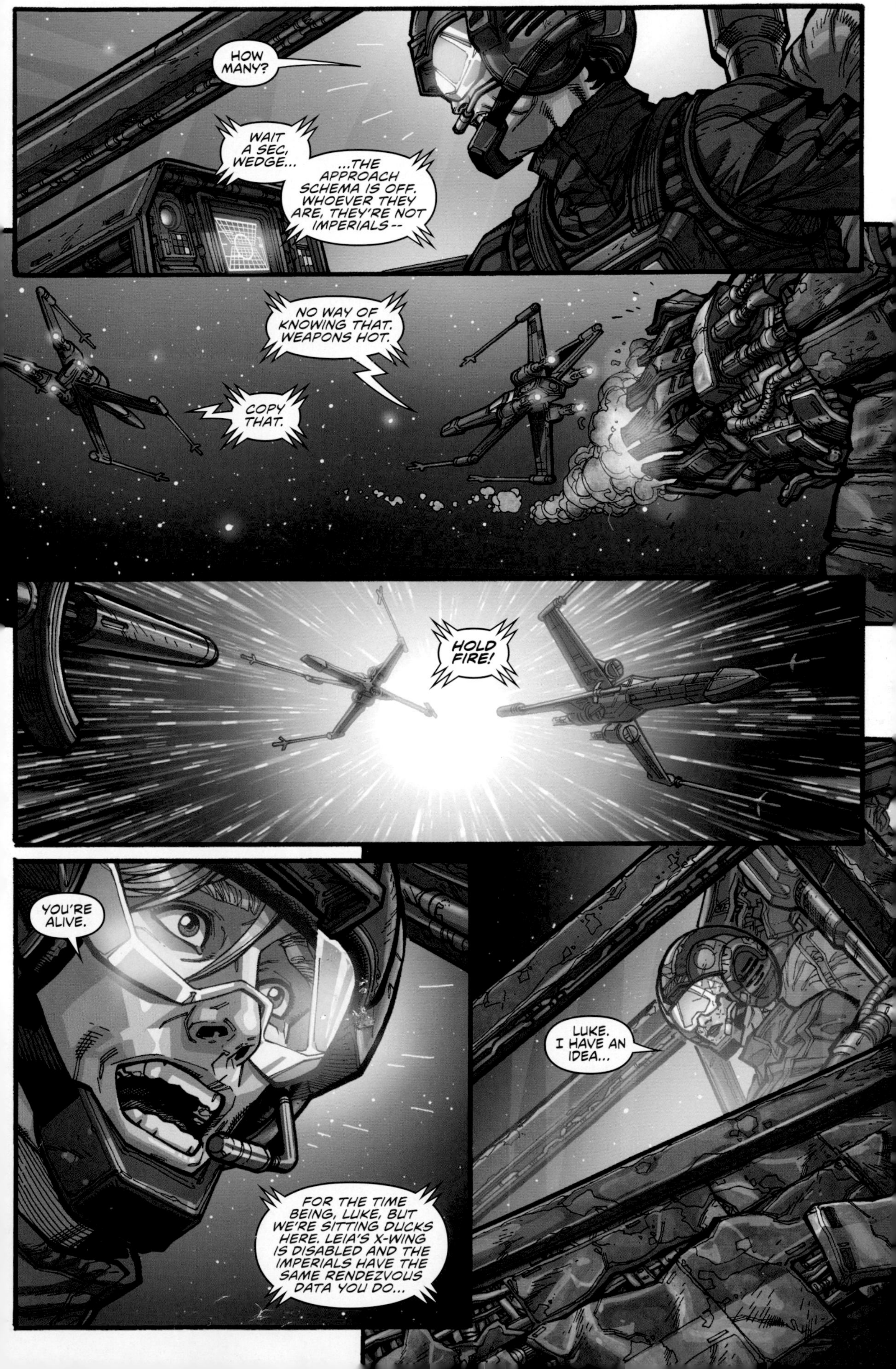
HOW MANY?
WAIT A SEC, WEDGE...
...THE APPROACH SCHEMA IS OFF. WHOEVER THEY ARE, THEY'RE NOT IMPERIALS --
NO WAY OF KNOWING THAT. WEAPONS HOT.
COPY THAT.
HOLD FIRE!
YOU'RE ALIVE.
FOR THE TIME BEING, LUKE, BUT WE'RE SITTING DUCKS HERE. LEIA'S X-WING IS DISABLED AND THE IMPERIALS HAVE THE SAME RENDEZVOUS DATA YOU DO...
LUKE. I HAVE AN IDEA...

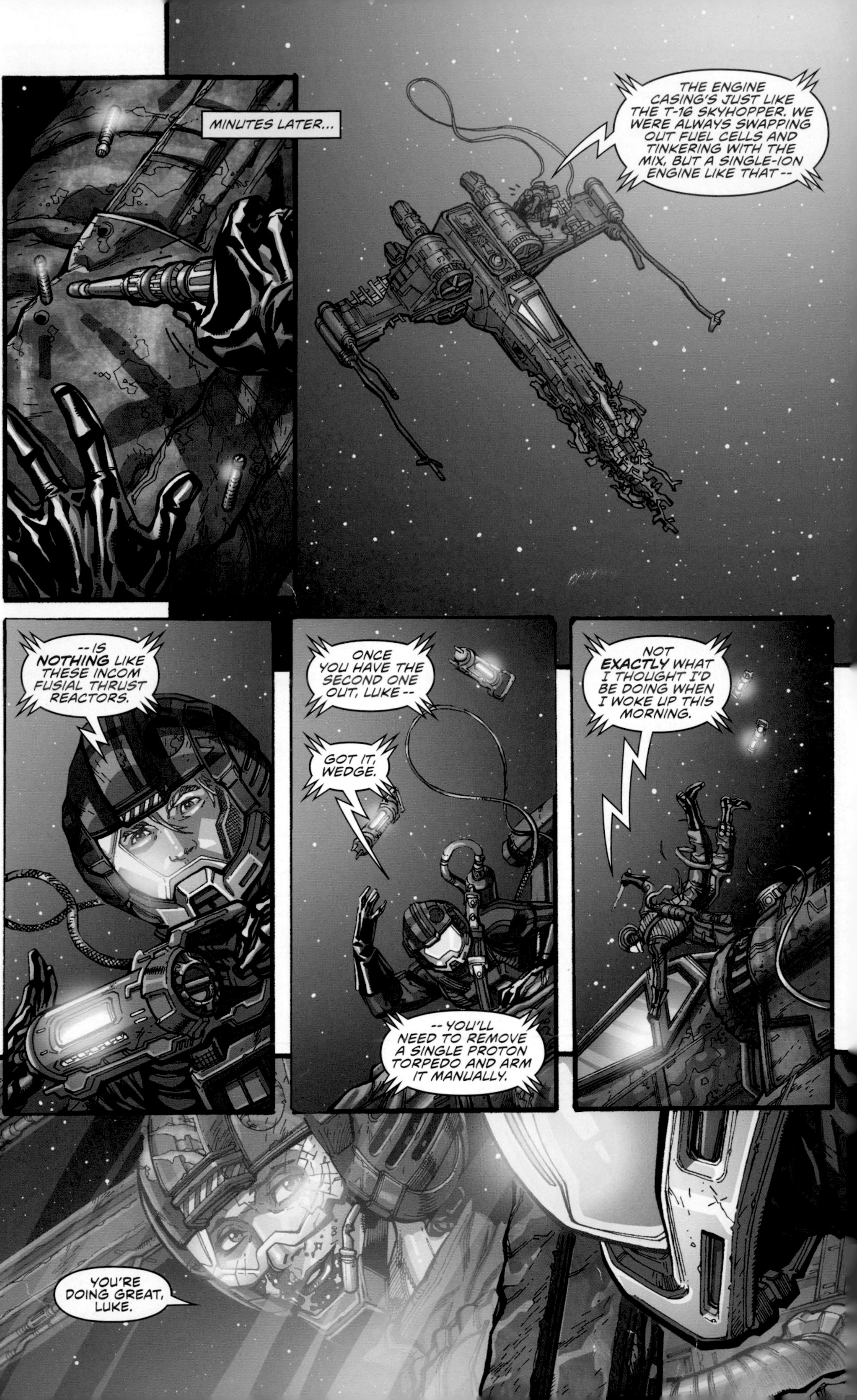
MINUTES LATER...
THE ENGINE CASING'S JUST LIKE THE T-16 SKYHOPPER. WE WERE ALWAYS SWAPPING OUT FUEL CELLS AND TINKERING WITH THE MIX, BUT A SINGLE-ION ENGINE LIKE THAT--
--IS NOTHING LIKE THESE INCOM FUSIAL THRUST REACTORS.
ONCE YOU HAVE THE SECOND ONE OUT, LUKE--
GOT IT, WEDGE.
--YOU'LL NEED TO REMOVE A SINGLE PROTON TORPEDO AND ARM IT MANUALLY.
NOT EXACTLY WHAT I THOUGHT I'D BE DOING WHEN I WOKE UP THIS MORNING.
YOU'RE DOING GREAT, LUKE.

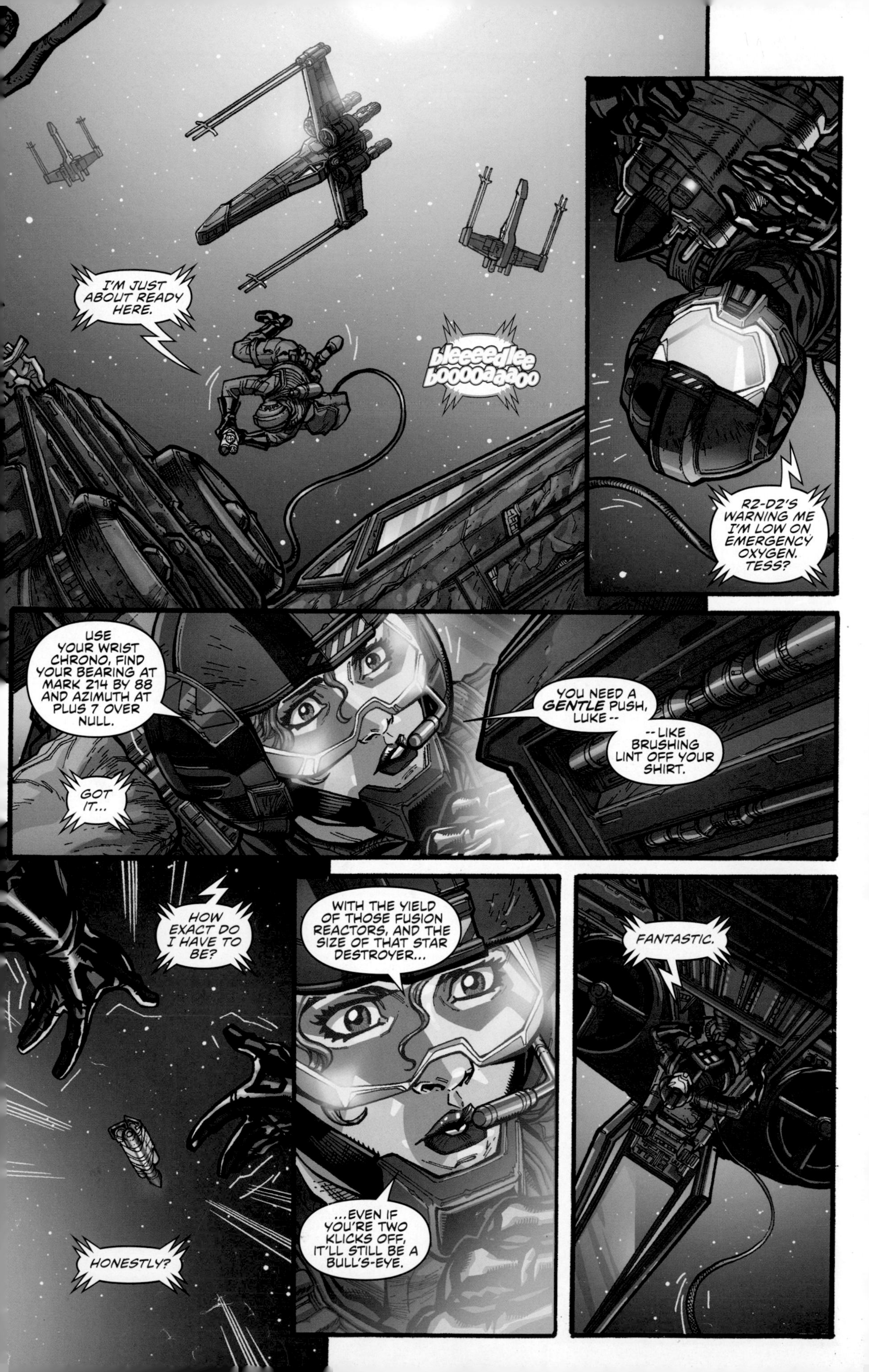
I'M JUST ABOUT READY HERE.
bleeeedlee boooaaaoo
R2-D2'S WARNING ME I'M LOW ON EMERGENCY OXYGEN. TESS?
USE YOUR WRIST CHRONO, FIND YOUR BEARING AT MARK 214 BY 88 AND AZIMUTH AT PLUS 7 OVER NULL.
GOT IT...
YOU NEED A GENTLE PUSH, LUKE --
-- LIKE BRUSHING LINT OFF YOUR SHIRT.
HOW EXACT DO I HAVE TO BE?
HONESTLY?
WITH THE YIELD OF THOSE FUSION REACTORS, AND THE SIZE OF THAT STAR DESTROYER...
...EVEN IF YOU'RE TWO KLICKS OFF, IT'LL STILL BE A BULL'S-EYE.
FANTASTIC.

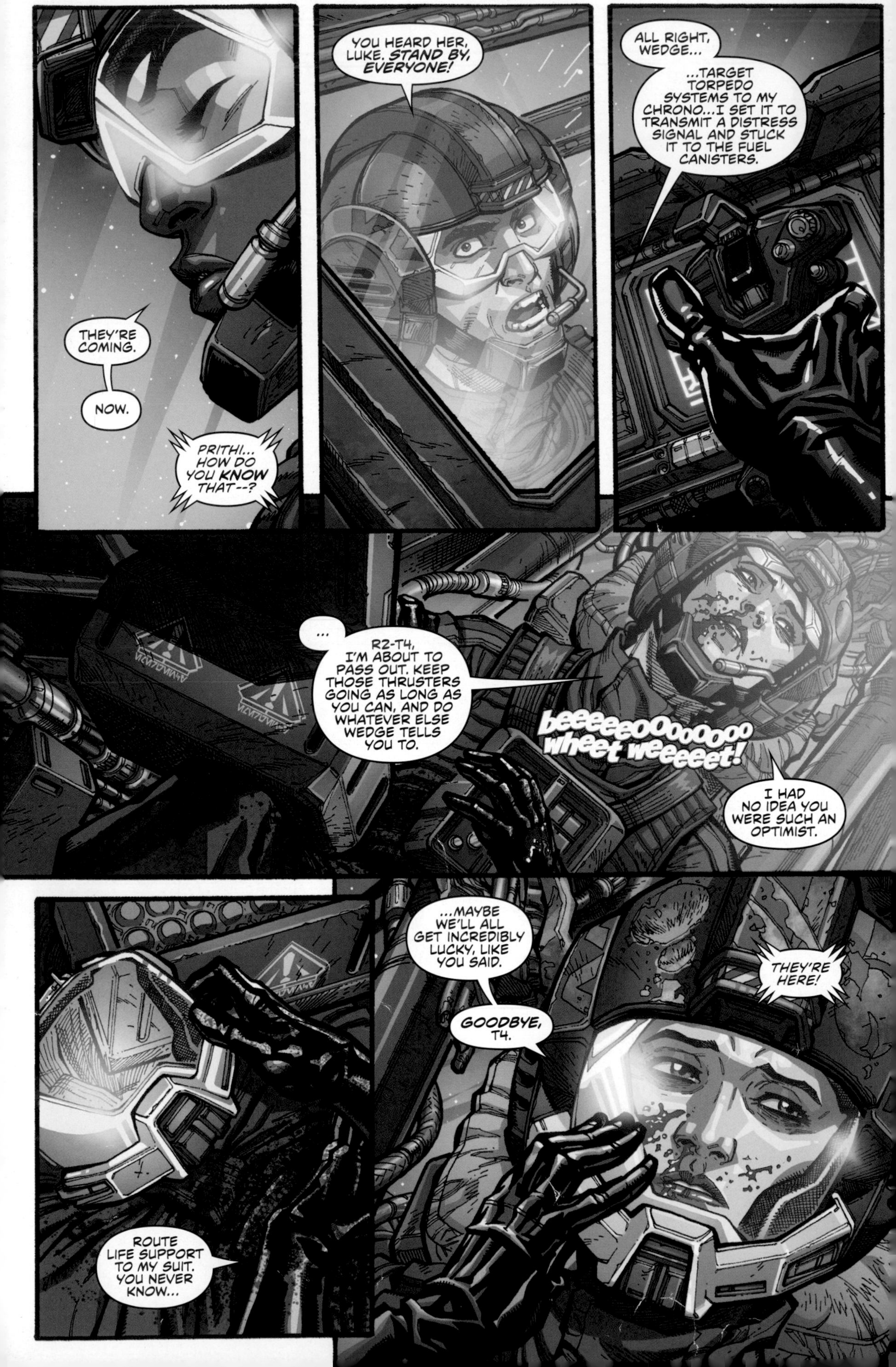
THEY'RE COMING.
NOW.
PRITHI... HOW DO YOU KNOW THAT--?
YOU HEARD HER, LUKE. STAND BY, EVERYONE!
ALL RIGHT, WEDGE...
...TARGET TORPEDO SYSTEMS TO MY CHRONO...I SET IT TO TRANSMIT A DISTRESS SIGNAL AND STUCK IT TO THE FUEL CANISTERS.
...
R2-T4, I'M ABOUT TO PASS OUT. KEEP THOSE THRUSTERS GOING AS LONG AS YOU CAN, AND DO WHATEVER ELSE WEDGE TELLS YOU TO.
beeeeeoooooooo wheet weeeeet!
I HAD NO IDEA YOU WERE SUCH AN OPTIMIST.
ROUTE LIFE SUPPORT TO MY SUIT. YOU NEVER KNOW...
...MAYBE WE'LL ALL GET INCREDIBLY LUCKY, LIKE YOU SAID.
GOODBYE, T4.
THEY'RE HERE!

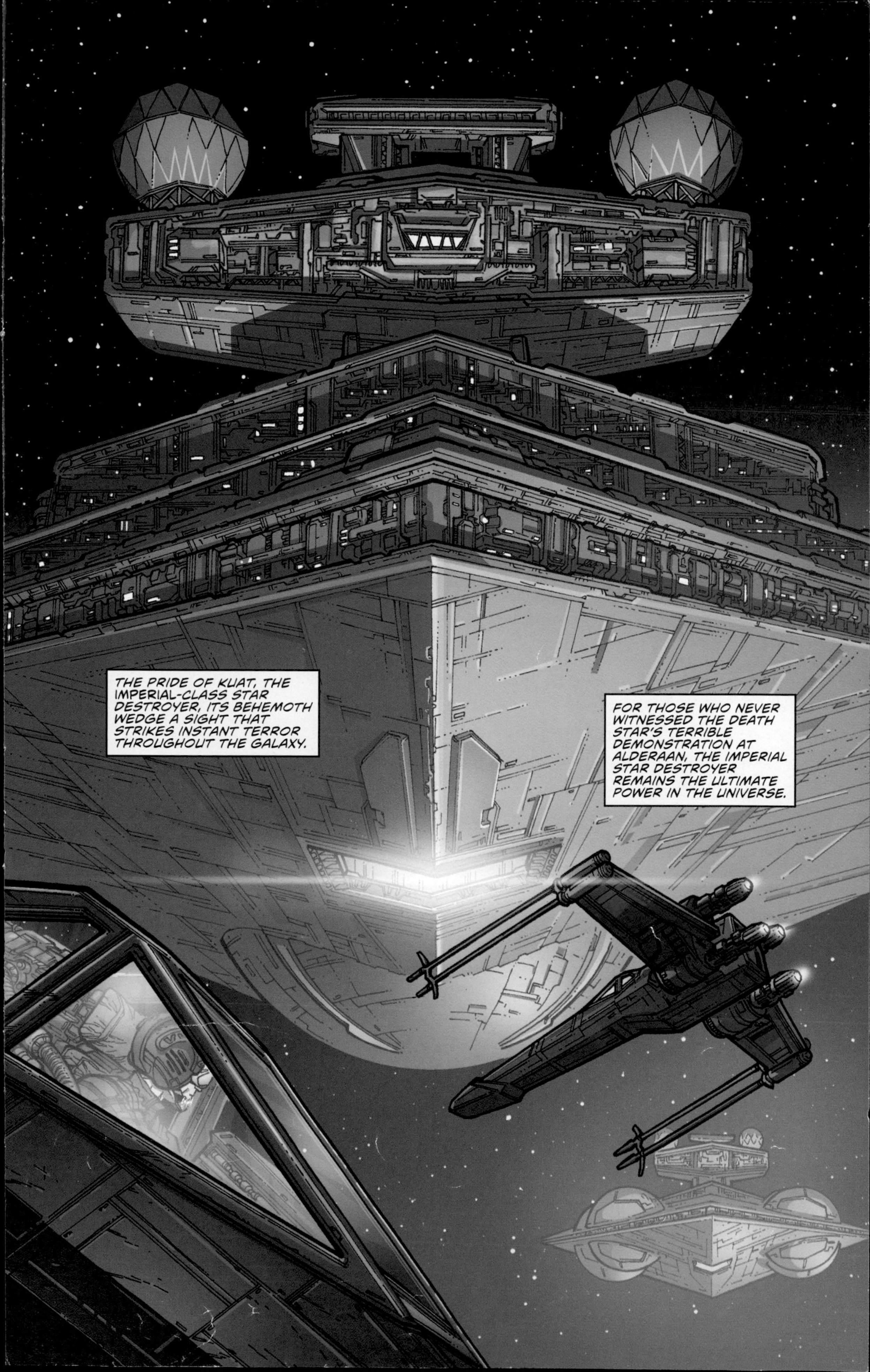
THE PRIDE OF KUAT, THE IMPERIAL-CLASS STAR DESTROYER, ITS BEHEMOTH WEDGE A SIGHT THAT STRIKES INSTANT TERROR THROUGHOUT THE GALAXY.
FOR THOSE WHO NEVER WITNESSED THE DEATH STAR'S TERRIBLE DEMONSTRATION AT ALDERAAN, THE IMPERIAL STAR DESTROYER REMAINS THE ULTIMATE POWER IN THE UNIVERSE.

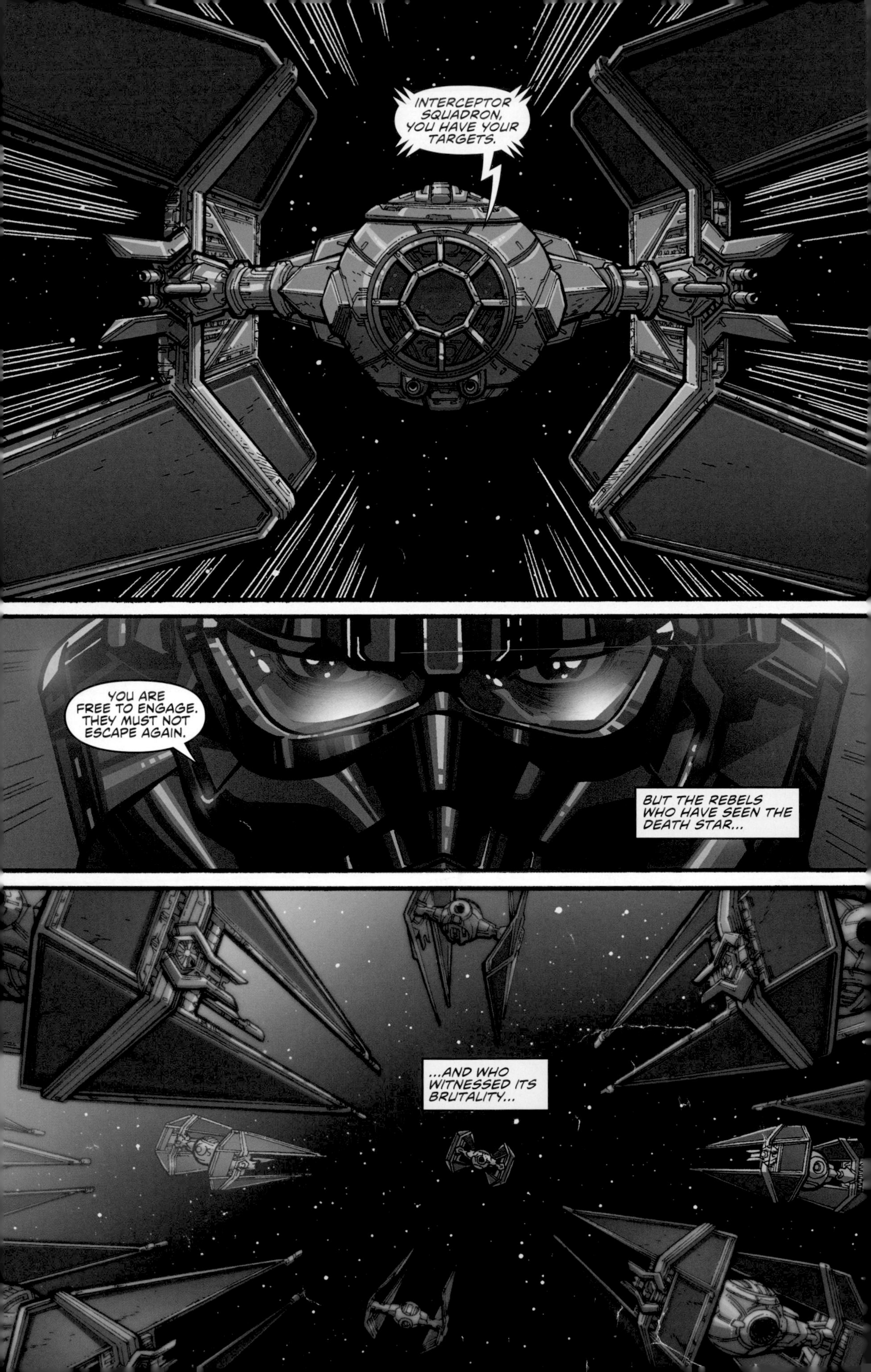
INTERCEPTOR SQUADRON, YOU HAVE YOUR TARGETS.
YOU ARE FREE TO ENGAGE. THEY MUST NOT ESCAPE AGAIN.
BUT THE REBELS WHO HAVE SEEN THE DEATH STAR...
...AND WHO WITNESSED ITS BRUTALITY...

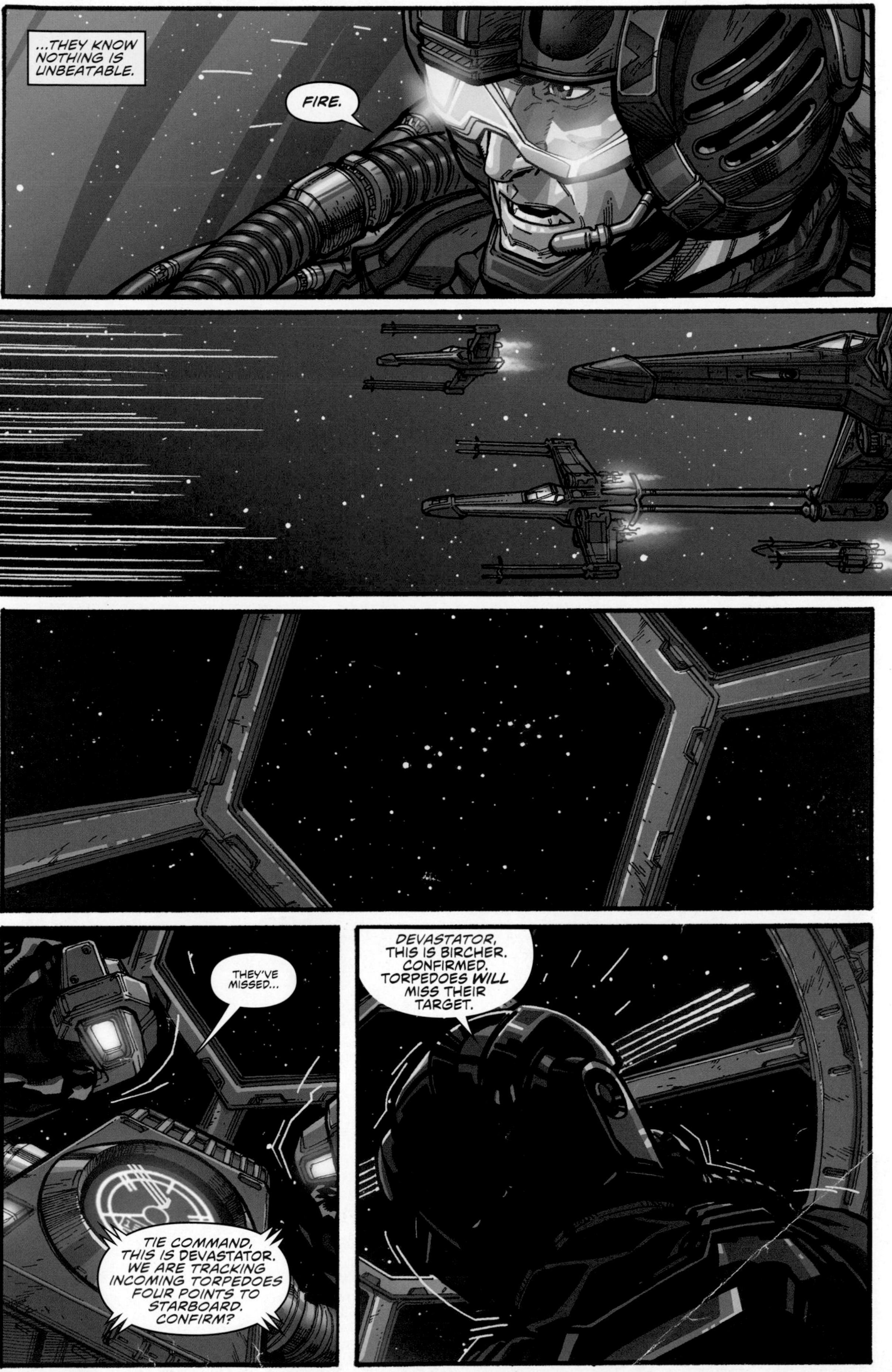
...THEY KNOW NOTHING IS UNBEATABLE.
FIRE.
THEY'VE MISSED...
TIE COMMAND, THIS IS DEVASTATOR. WE ARE TRACKING INCOMING TORPEDOES FOUR POINTS TO STARBOARD. CONFIRM?
DEVASTATOR, THIS IS BIRCHER. CONFIRMED. TORPEDOES WILL MISS THEIR TARGET.

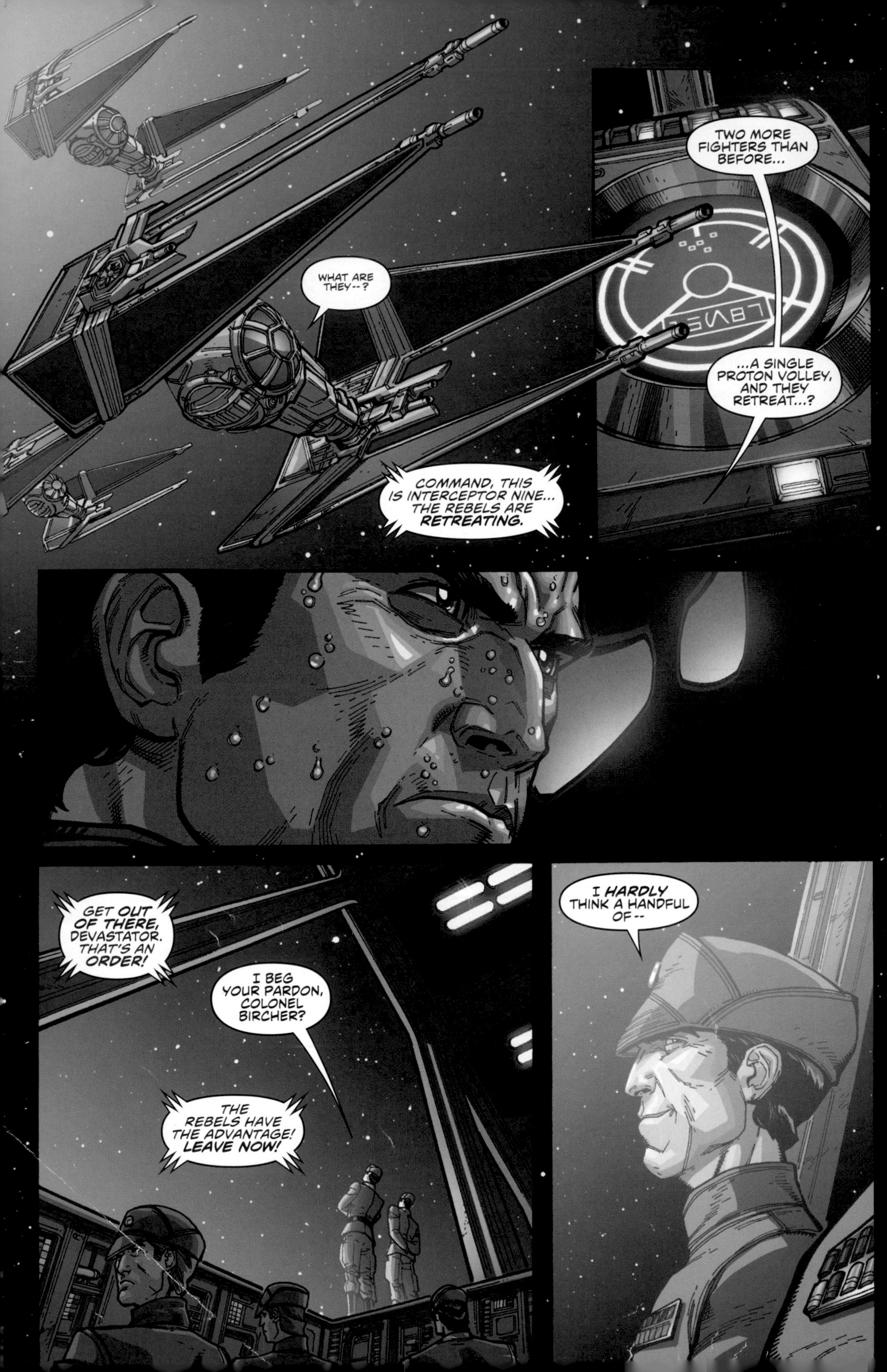
WHAT ARE THEY--?
COMMAND, THIS IS INTERCEPTOR NINE... THE REBELS ARE **RETREATING**.
TWO MORE FIGHTERS THAN BEFORE...
...A SINGLE PROTON VOLLEY, AND THEY RETREAT...?
GET **OUT OF THERE**, DEVASTATOR. THAT'S AN **ORDER**!
I BEG YOUR PARDON, COLONEL BIRCHER?
THE REBELS HAVE THE ADVANTAGE! **LEAVE NOW!**
I **HARDLY** THINK A HANDFUL OF--

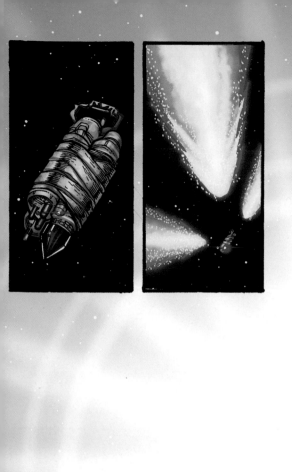

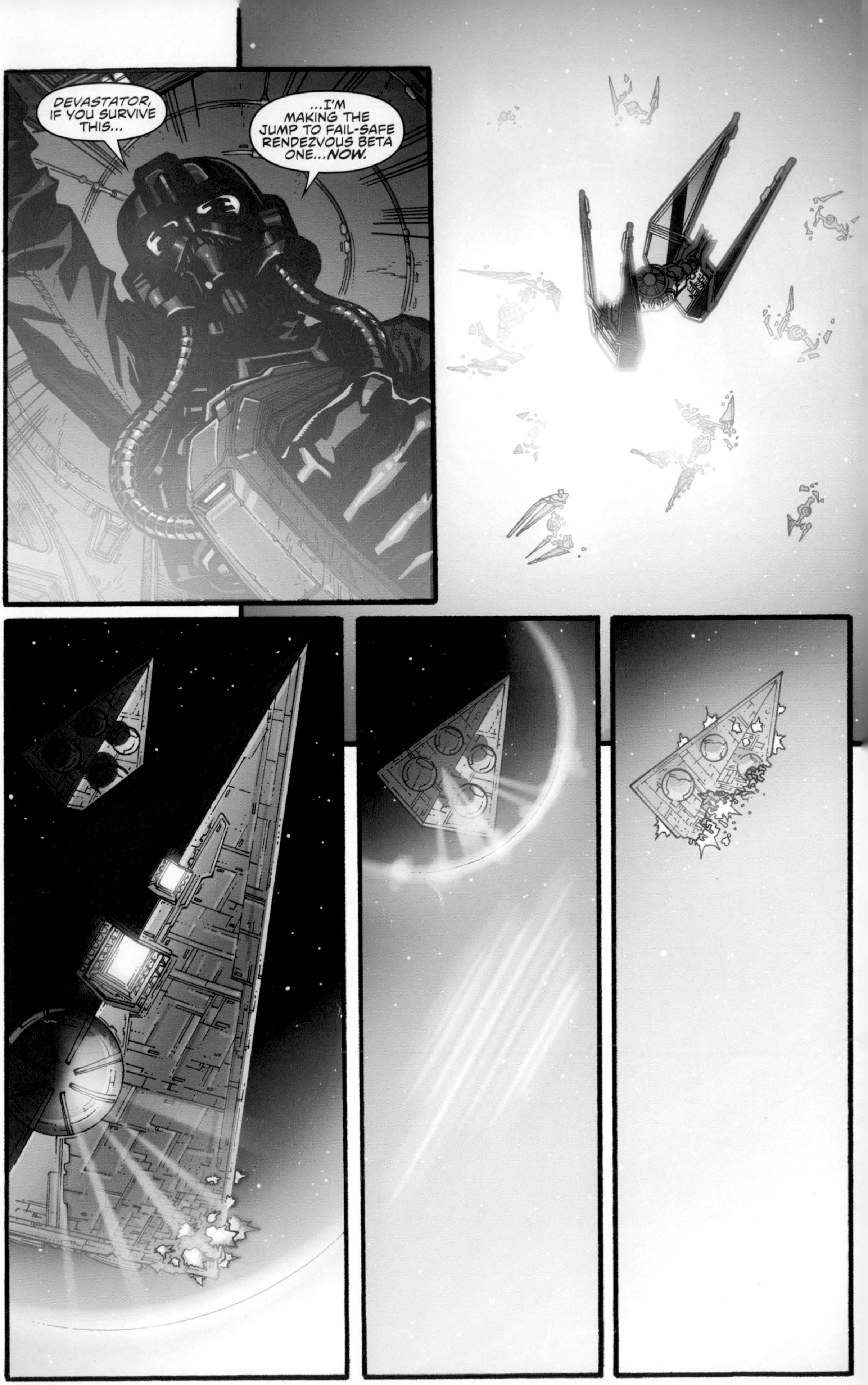
DEVASTATOR, IF YOU SURVIVE THIS...
...I'M MAKING THE JUMP TO FAIL-SAFE RENDEZVOUS BETA ONE...NOW.

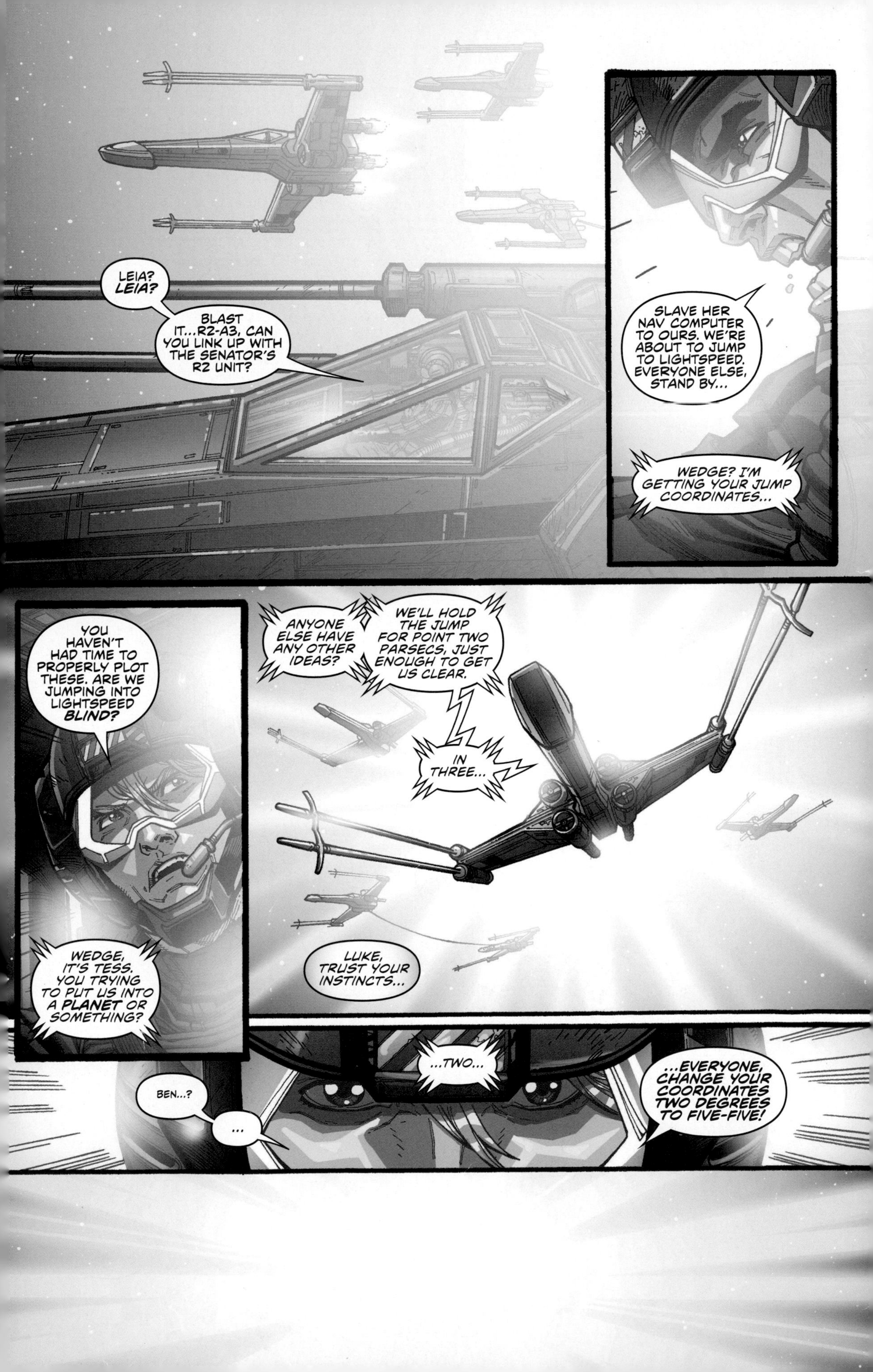

LEIA? LEIA?
BLAST IT...R2-A3, CAN YOU LINK UP WITH THE SENATOR'S R2 UNIT?
SLAVE HER NAV COMPUTER TO OURS. WE'RE ABOUT TO JUMP TO LIGHTSPEED. EVERYONE ELSE, STAND BY...
WEDGE? I'M GETTING YOUR JUMP COORDINATES...
YOU HAVEN'T HAD TIME TO PROPERLY PLOT THESE. ARE WE JUMPING INTO LIGHTSPEED BLIND?
ANYONE ELSE HAVE ANY OTHER IDEAS?
WE'LL HOLD THE JUMP FOR POINT TWO PARSECS, JUST ENOUGH TO GET US CLEAR.
IN THREE...
WEDGE, IT'S TESS. YOU TRYING TO PUT US INTO A PLANET OR SOMETHING?
LUKE, TRUST YOUR INSTINCTS...
BEN...?
...
...TWO...
...EVERYONE, CHANGE YOUR COORDINATES TWO DEGREES TO FIVE-FIVE!

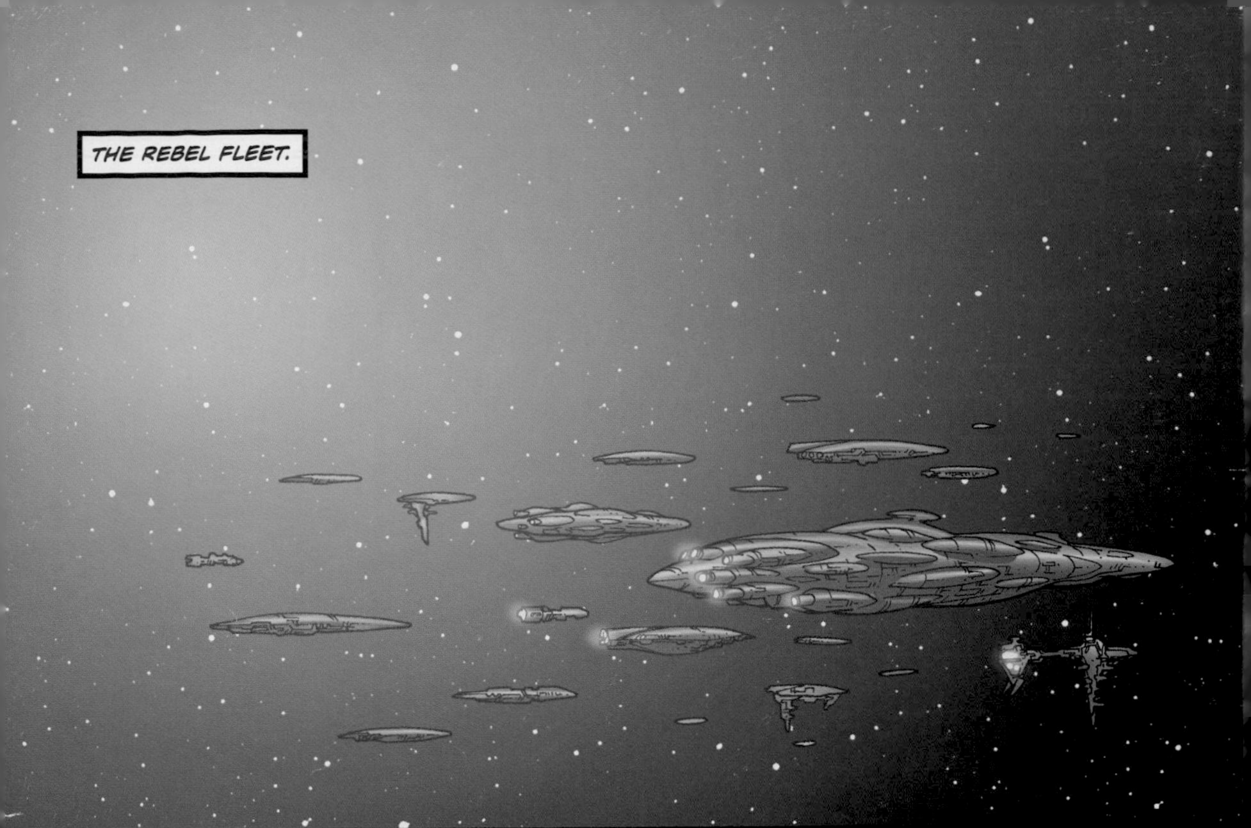
THE REBEL FLEET.

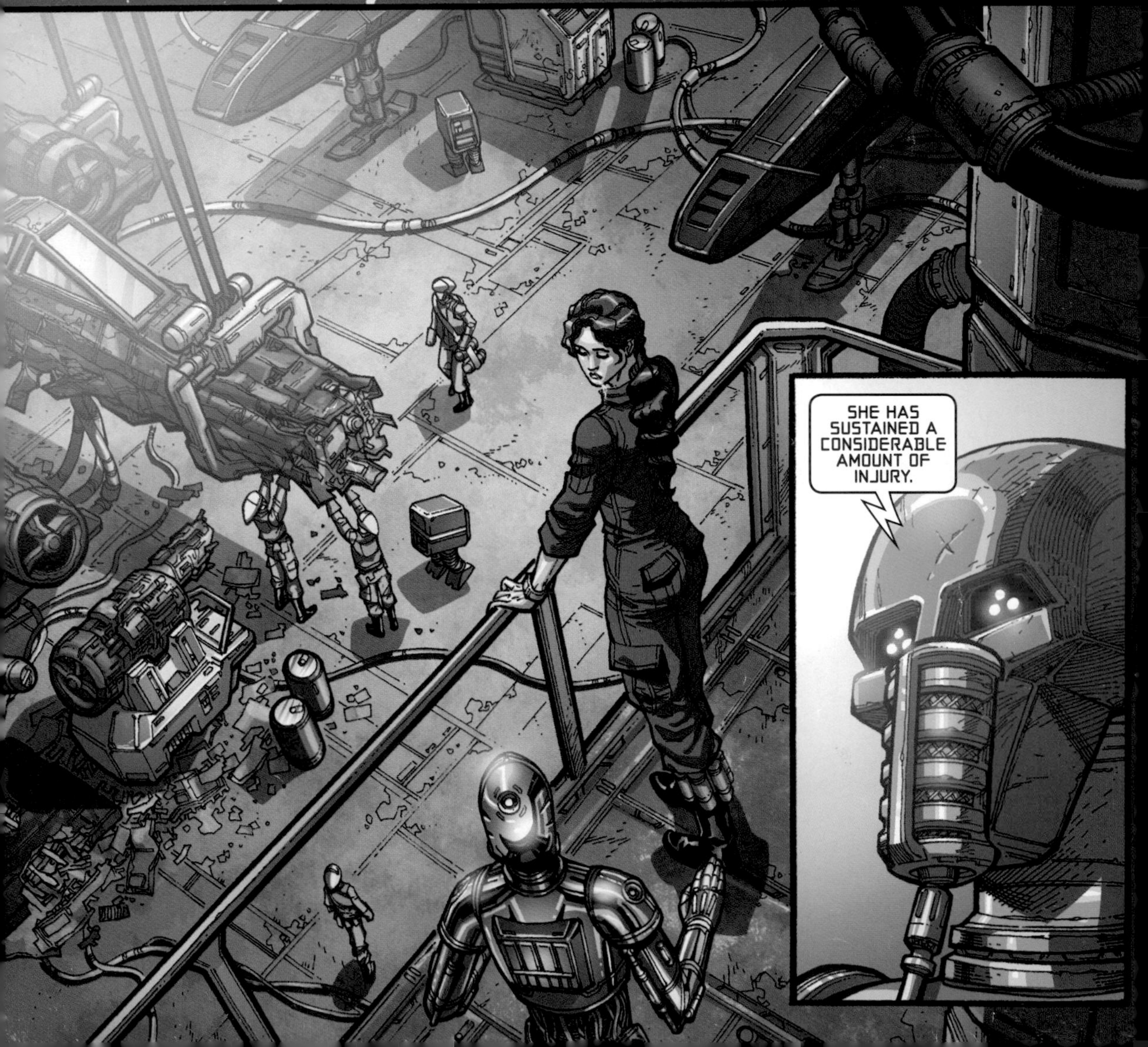
SHE HAS SUSTAINED A CONSIDERABLE AMOUNT OF INJURY.

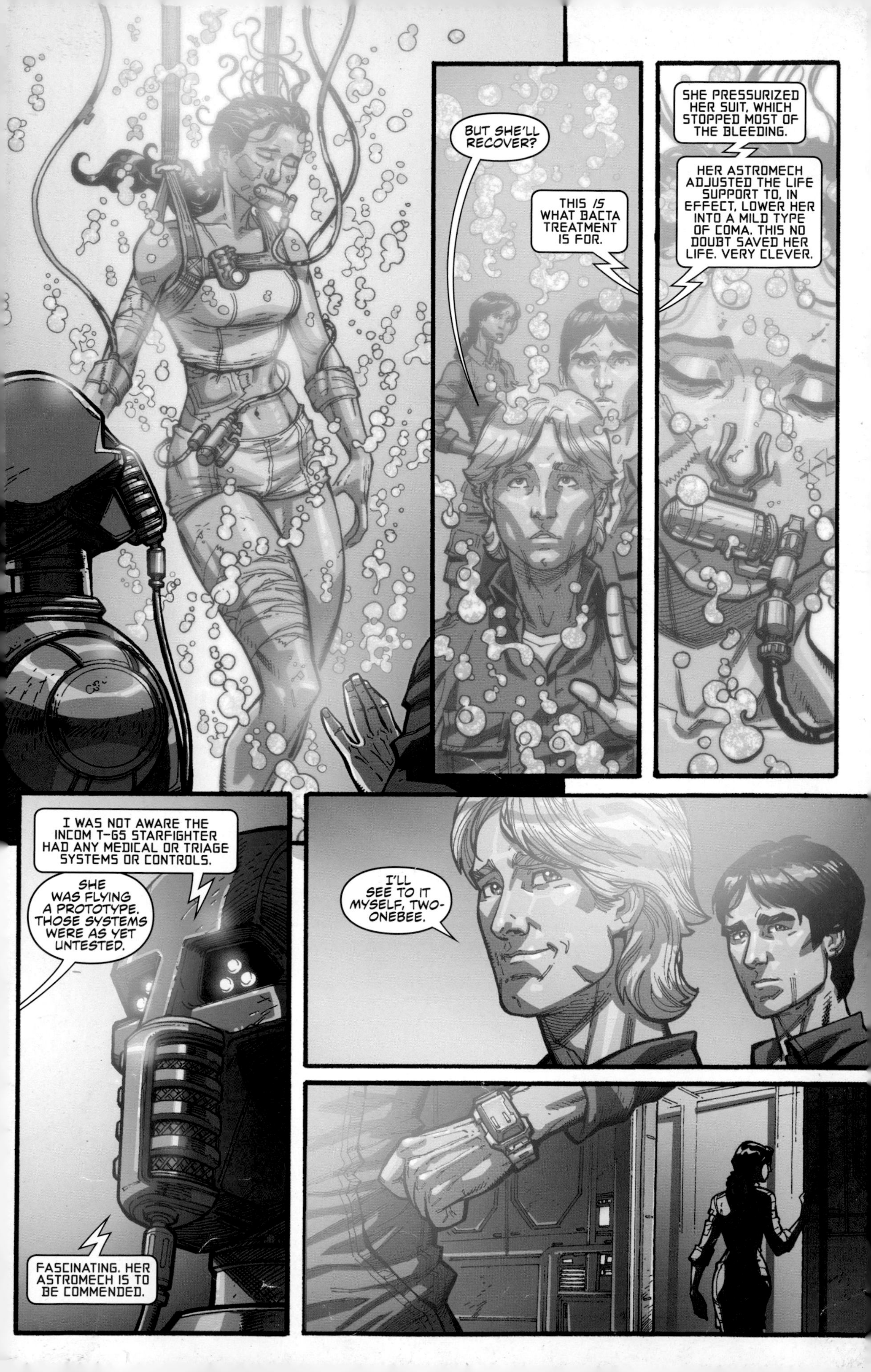
BUT SHE'LL RECOVER?
THIS *IS* WHAT BACTA TREATMENT IS FOR.
SHE PRESSURIZED HER SUIT, WHICH STOPPED MOST OF THE BLEEDING.
HER ASTROMECH ADJUSTED THE LIFE SUPPORT TO, IN EFFECT, LOWER HER INTO A MILD TYPE OF COMA. THIS NO DOUBT SAVED HER LIFE. VERY CLEVER.
I WAS NOT AWARE THE INCOM T-65 STARFIGHTER HAD ANY MEDICAL OR TRIAGE SYSTEMS OR CONTROLS.
SHE WAS FLYING A PROTOTYPE. THOSE SYSTEMS WERE AS YET UNTESTED.
FASCINATING. HER ASTROMECH IS TO BE COMMENDED.
I'LL SEE TO IT MYSELF, TWO-ONEBEE.

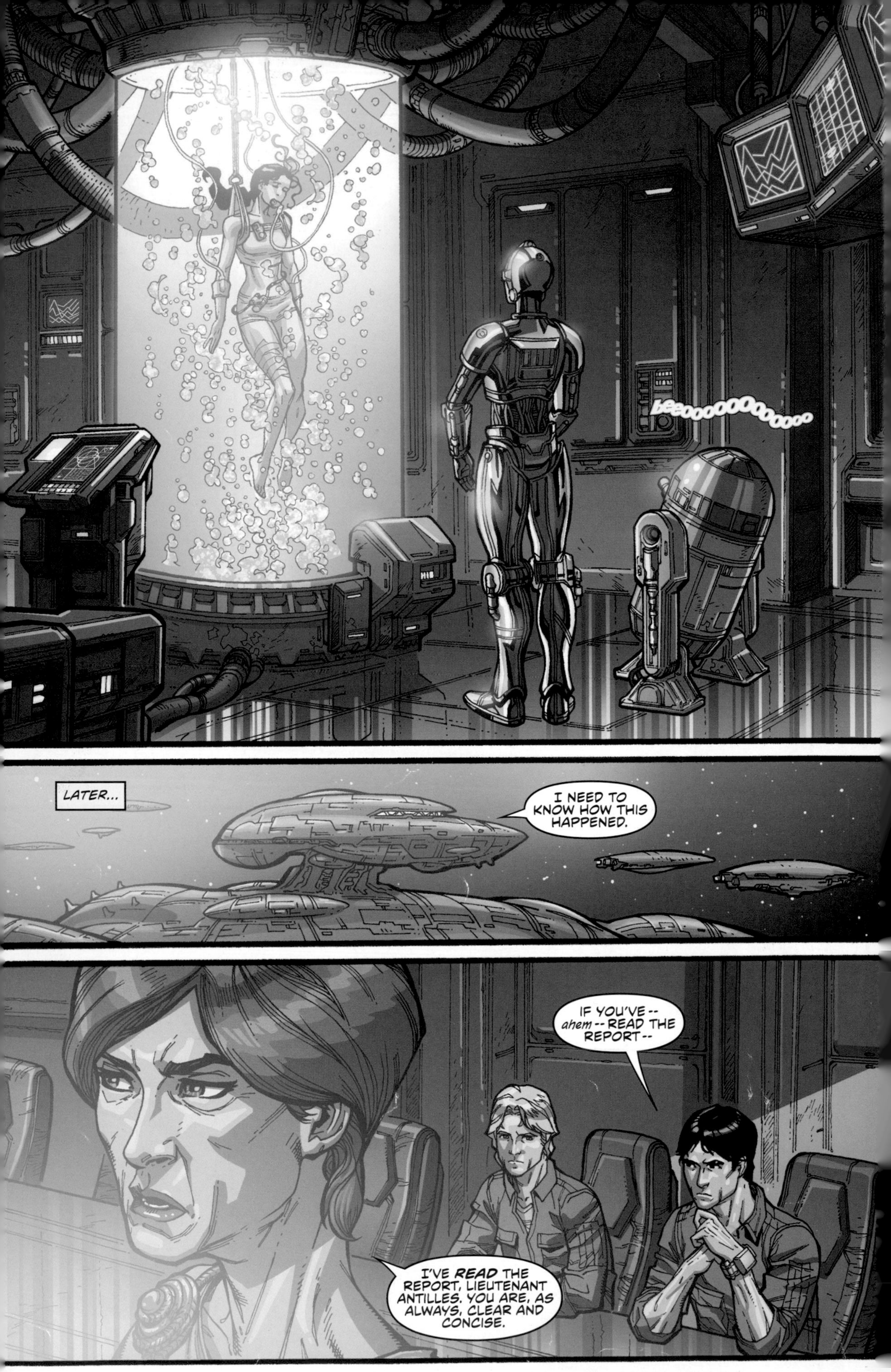
beeooooOOOOooooo
LATER...
I NEED TO KNOW HOW THIS HAPPENED.
IF YOU'VE -- *ahem* -- READ THE REPORT --
I'VE **READ** THE REPORT, LIEUTENANT ANTILLES. YOU ARE, AS ALWAYS, CLEAR AND CONCISE.

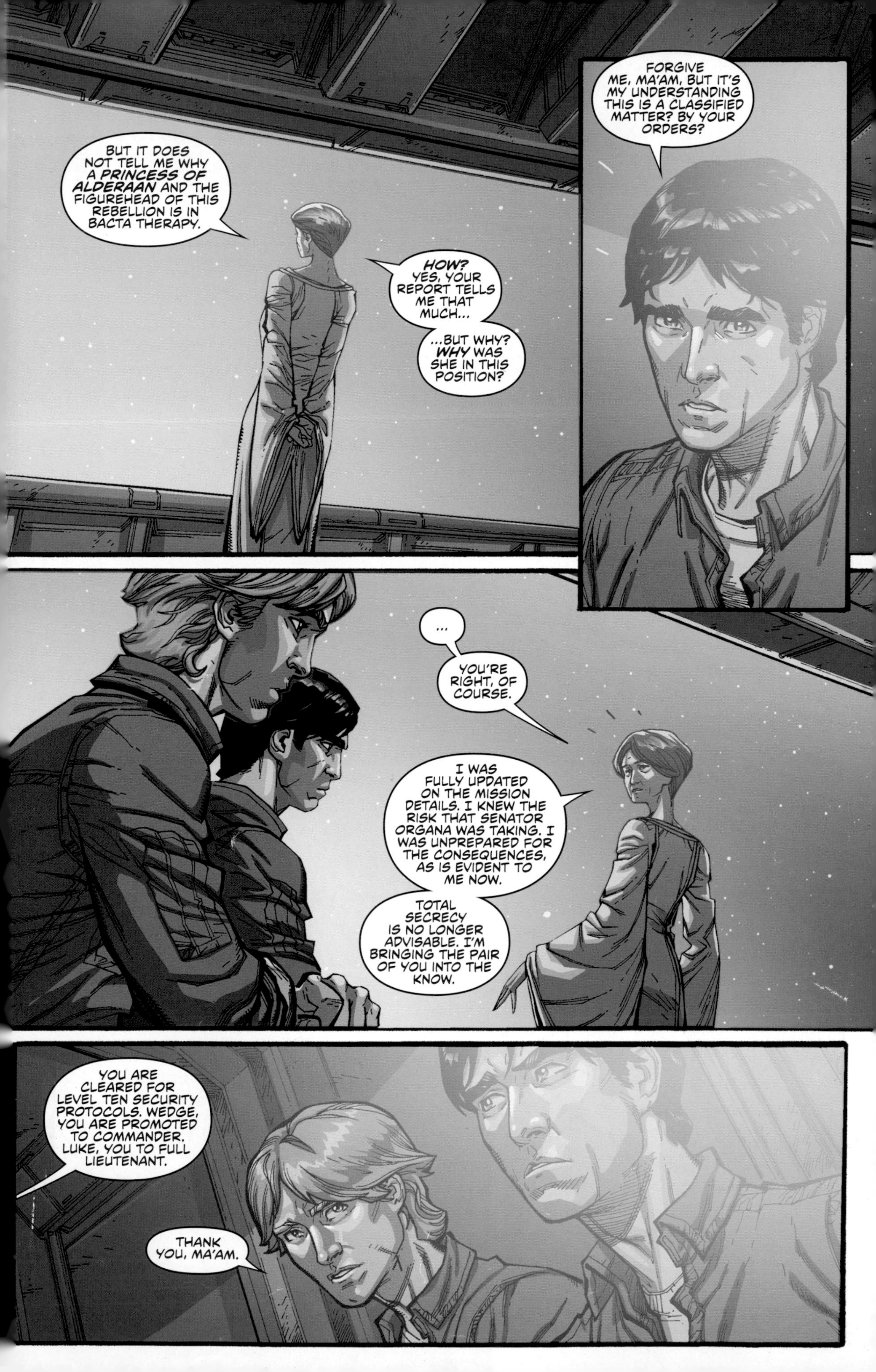
BUT IT DOES NOT TELL ME WHY A *PRINCESS OF ALDERAAN* AND THE FIGUREHEAD OF THIS REBELLION IS IN BACTA THERAPY.
HOW? YES, YOUR REPORT TELLS ME THAT MUCH...
...BUT WHY? *WHY* WAS SHE IN THIS POSITION?
FORGIVE ME, MA'AM, BUT IT'S MY UNDERSTANDING THIS IS A CLASSIFIED MATTER? BY YOUR ORDERS?
...
YOU'RE RIGHT, OF COURSE.
I WAS FULLY UPDATED ON THE MISSION DETAILS. I KNEW THE RISK THAT SENATOR ORGANA WAS TAKING. I WAS UNPREPARED FOR THE CONSEQUENCES, AS IS EVIDENT TO ME NOW.
TOTAL SECRECY IS NO LONGER ADVISABLE. I'M BRINGING THE PAIR OF YOU INTO THE KNOW.
YOU ARE CLEARED FOR LEVEL TEN SECURITY PROTOCOLS. WEDGE, YOU ARE PROMOTED TO COMMANDER. LUKE, YOU TO FULL LIEUTENANT.
THANK YOU, MA'AM.

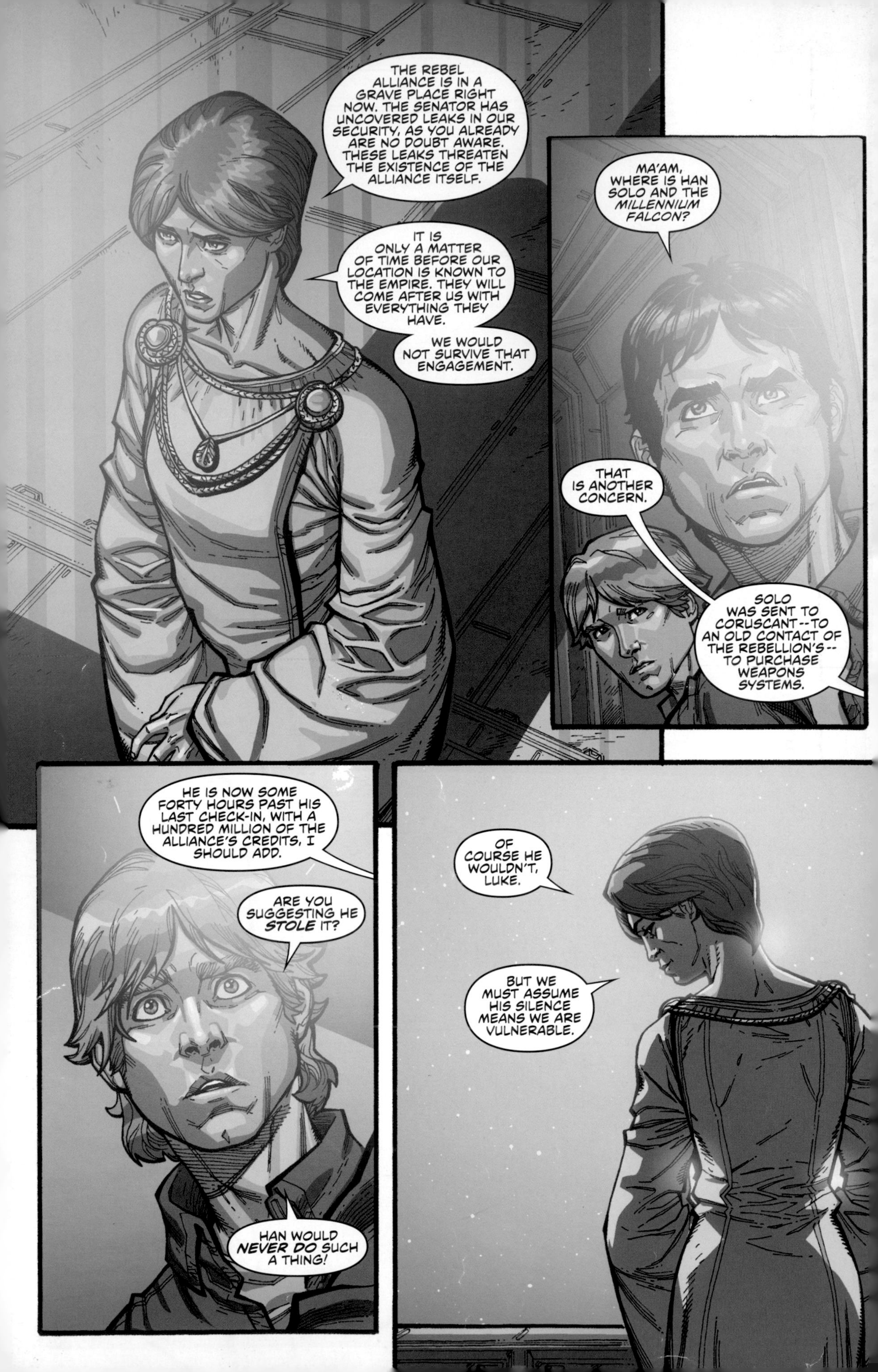
THE REBEL ALLIANCE IS IN A GRAVE PLACE RIGHT NOW. THE SENATOR HAS UNCOVERED LEAKS IN OUR SECURITY, AS YOU ALREADY ARE NO DOUBT AWARE. THESE LEAKS THREATEN THE EXISTENCE OF THE ALLIANCE ITSELF.
IT IS ONLY A MATTER OF TIME BEFORE OUR LOCATION IS KNOWN TO THE EMPIRE. THEY WILL COME AFTER US WITH EVERYTHING THEY HAVE.
WE WOULD NOT SURVIVE THAT ENGAGEMENT.
MA'AM, WHERE IS HAN SOLO AND THE *MILLENNIUM FALCON*?
THAT IS ANOTHER CONCERN.
SOLO WAS SENT TO CORUSCANT--TO AN OLD CONTACT OF THE REBELLION'S--TO PURCHASE WEAPONS SYSTEMS.
HE IS NOW SOME FORTY HOURS PAST HIS LAST CHECK-IN, WITH A HUNDRED MILLION OF THE ALLIANCE'S CREDITS, I SHOULD ADD.
ARE YOU SUGGESTING HE ***STOLE*** IT?
HAN WOULD ***NEVER DO*** SUCH A THING!
OF COURSE HE WOULDN'T, LUKE.
BUT WE MUST ASSUME HIS SILENCE MEANS WE ARE VULNERABLE.

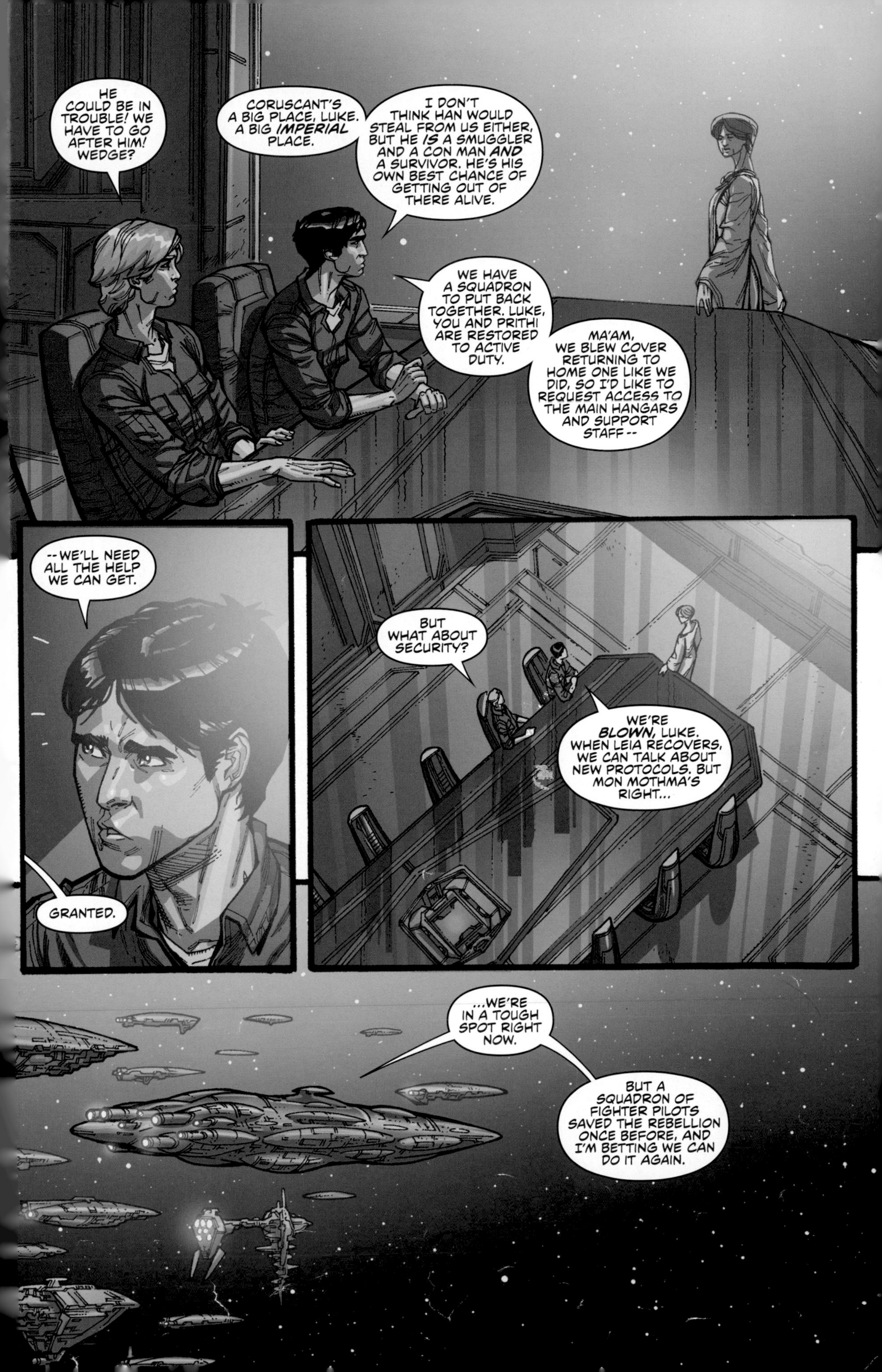

HE COULD BE IN TROUBLE! WE HAVE TO GO AFTER HIM! WEDGE?
CORUSCANT'S A BIG PLACE, LUKE. A BIG *IMPERIAL* PLACE.
I DON'T THINK HAN WOULD STEAL FROM US EITHER, BUT HE *IS* A SMUGGLER AND A CON MAN *AND* A SURVIVOR. HE'S HIS OWN BEST CHANCE OF GETTING OUT OF THERE ALIVE.
WE HAVE A SQUADRON TO PUT BACK TOGETHER. LUKE, YOU AND PRITHI ARE RESTORED TO ACTIVE DUTY.
MA'AM, WE BLEW COVER RETURNING TO HOME ONE LIKE WE DID, SO I'D LIKE TO REQUEST ACCESS TO THE MAIN HANGARS AND SUPPORT STAFF --
-- WE'LL NEED ALL THE HELP WE CAN GET.
GRANTED.
BUT WHAT ABOUT SECURITY?
WE'RE *BLOWN,* LUKE. WHEN LEIA RECOVERS, WE CAN TALK ABOUT NEW PROTOCOLS. BUT MON MOTHMA'S RIGHT...
...WE'RE IN A TOUGH SPOT RIGHT NOW.
BUT A SQUADRON OF FIGHTER PILOTS SAVED THE REBELLION ONCE BEFORE, AND I'M BETTING WE CAN DO IT AGAIN.

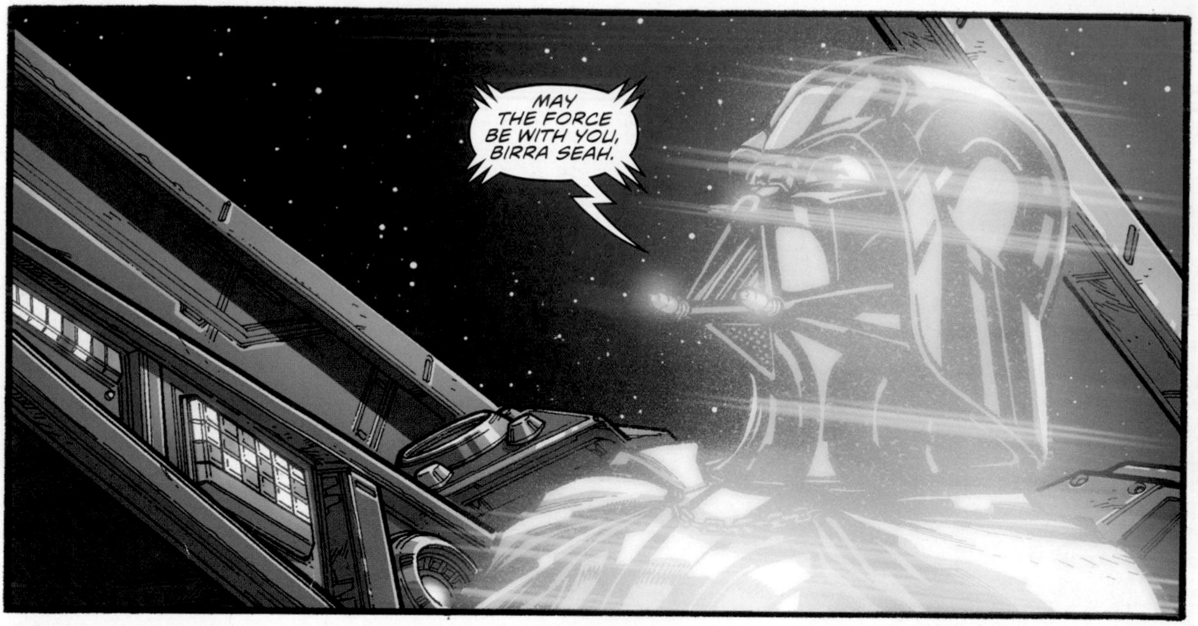
MAY THE FORCE BE WITH YOU, BIRRA SEAH.

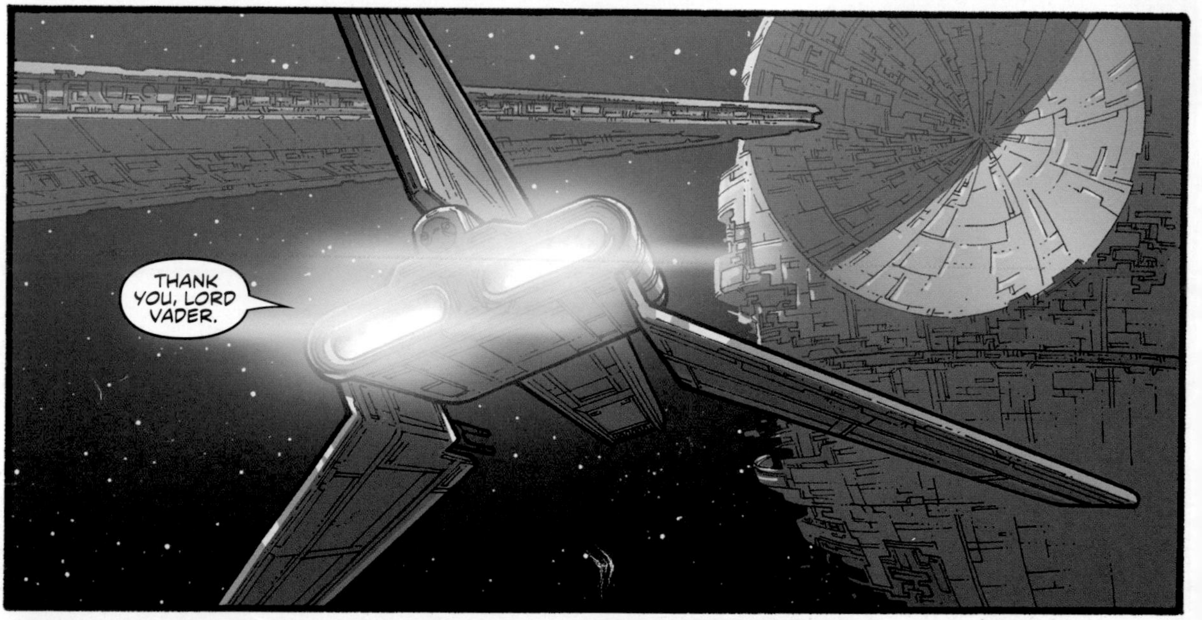
THANK YOU, LORD VADER.

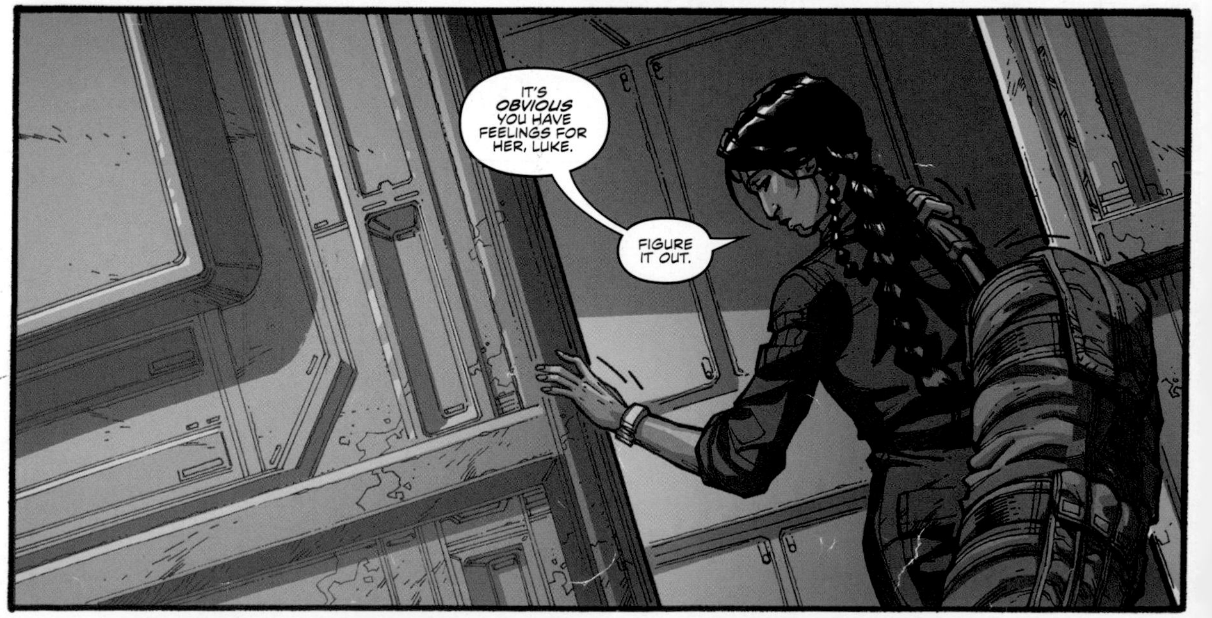
IT'S *OBVIOUS* YOU HAVE FEELINGS FOR HER, LUKE.
FIGURE IT OUT.

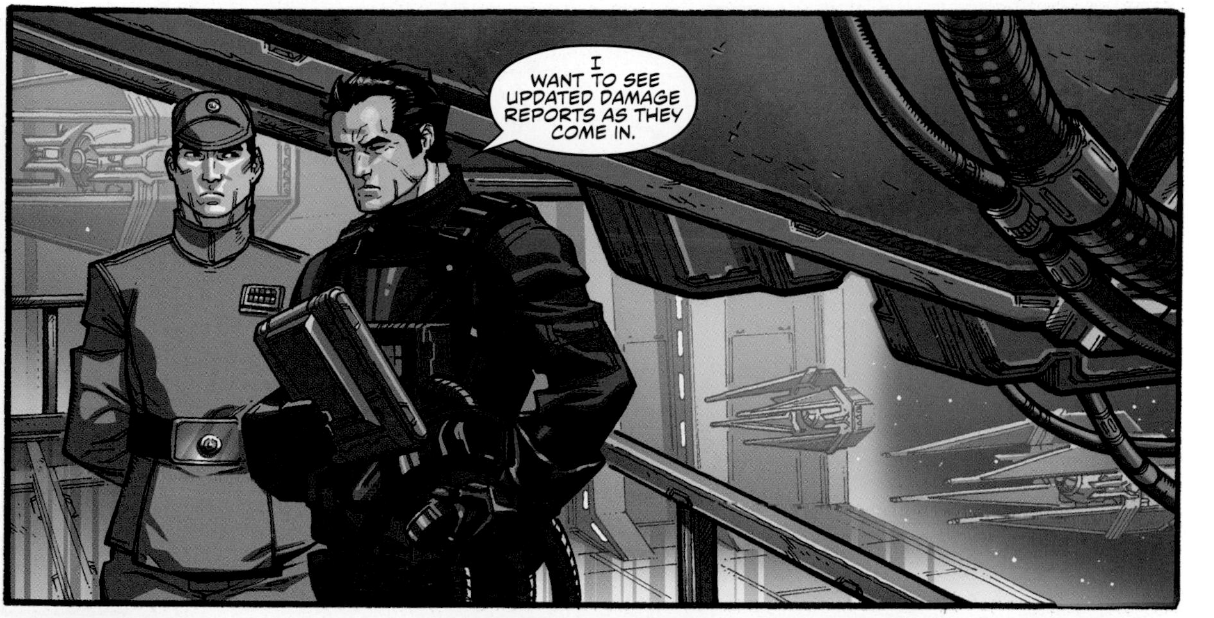
I WANT TO SEE UPDATED DAMAGE REPORTS AS THEY COME IN.
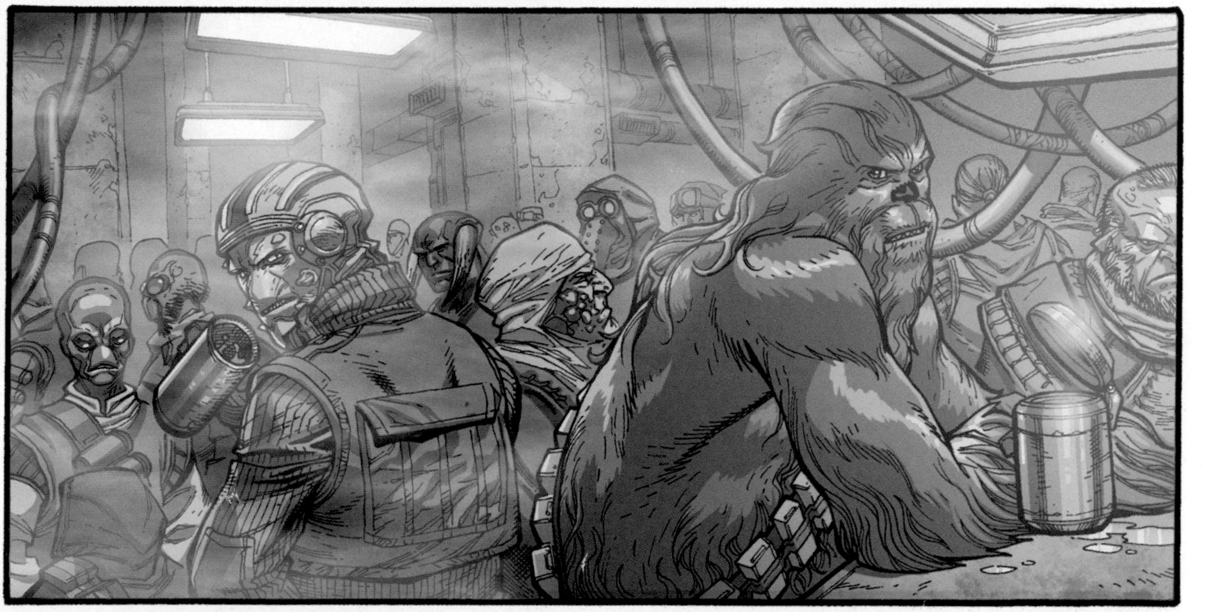
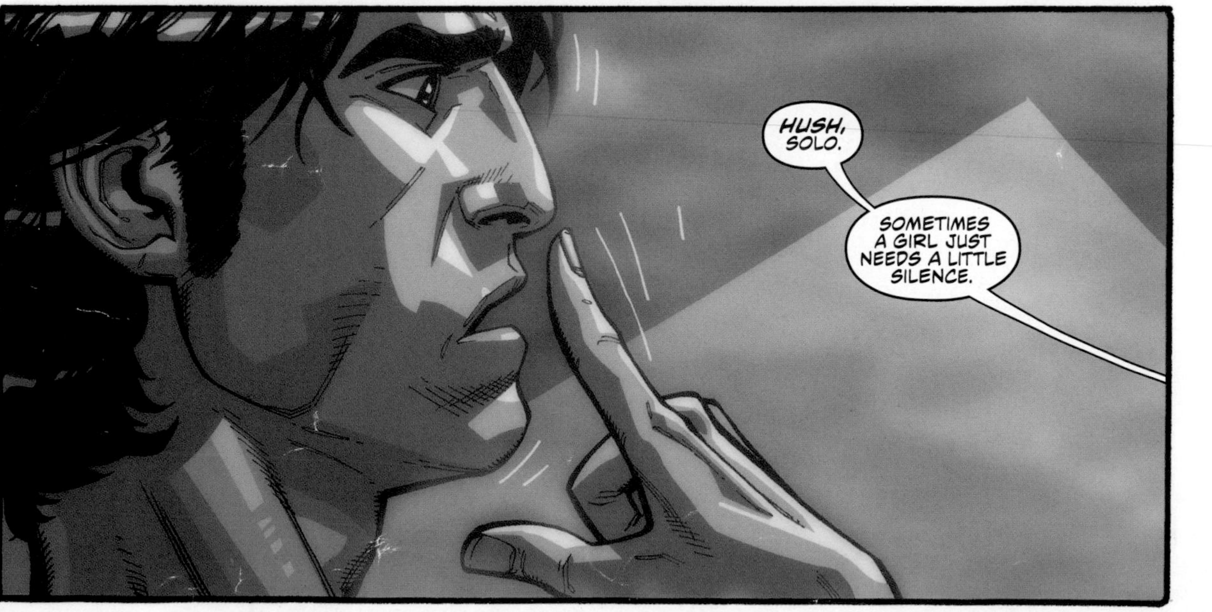
HUSH, SOLO.
SOMETIMES A GIRL JUST NEEDS A LITTLE SILENCE.

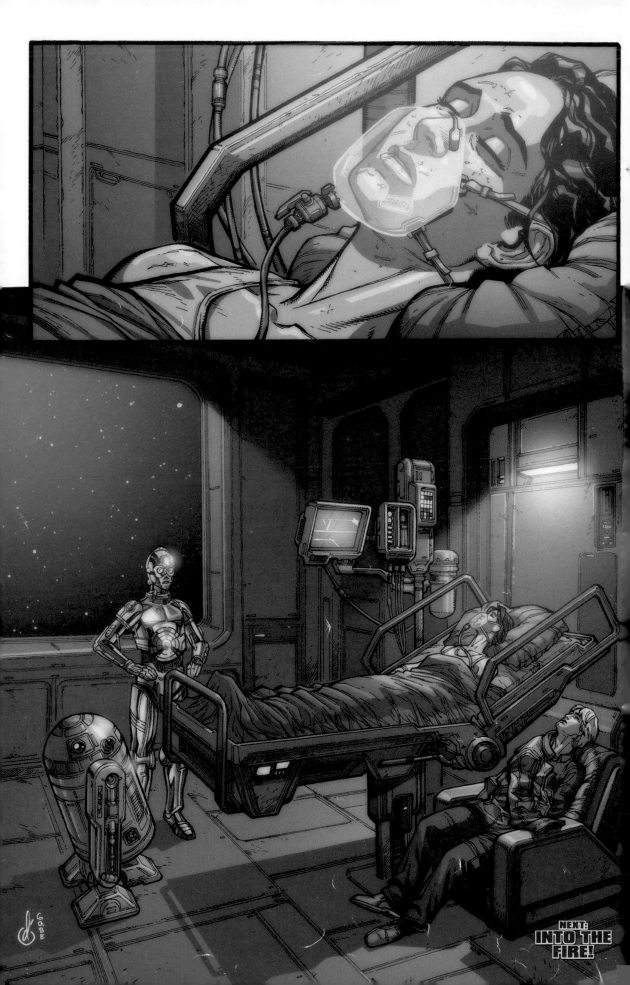

NEXT: INTO THE FIRE!